Tails on the Hill

Stories about a Family and Its Dogs

Carol Thornton

illustrations by Vicky Williams Harrison

A Chaparral Book for Young Readers

TCU PRESS

Fort Worth, Texas

Library of Congress Cataloging-in-Publication Data

Thornton, Carol, 1929-
Tails on the hill : stories about a family and its dogs / Carol Thornton ; illustrated by Vicky Williams Harrison.
p. cm. - (Chaparral books for young readers)
ISBN 978-0-87565-573-4 (alk. paper)
1. Dogs--Texas, West--Fiction. 2. Human-animal relationships--Fiction. 3. Farm life--Texas, West--Fiction. 4. Families--Texas, West--Fiction. 5. Texas, West--Fiction. I. Harrison, Vicky Williams, 1950- illustrator. II. Title. III. Chaparral book for young readers
PS3620.H7828T35 2013
813'.6--dc23
2013014542

Text design by Rebecca A. Allen

TCU Press
TCU Box 298300
Fort Worth, Texas 76129
817.257.7822
www.prs.tcu.edu

To order books call 1.800.826.8911

Contents

Prologue

Mornings started with a slight breeze, but by noon that breeze would become a gale. The wind would blow hard from the south and the next day it would blow hard from the north, but every day it blew hard from somewhere. I'd stand at the kitchen window and watch Mother's sheets whip around and around the clothesline and the dog pans bang and bump doing cartwheels across the yard till they all piled up against the fence. My daddy always said that was just part of living in West Texas.

Mother and Daddy met each other in college and I guess that's when they fell in love 'cause they got married and Daddy took Mother to Olney. Mother said she had to make a lot of changes, moving from a big city like Fort Worth to a small town. She said it wasn't easy—like she didn't know she shouldn't wear shorts to the grocery store and she thought the neighbors were a little too nosy. Daddy said they were just being friendly.

He and Mother were driving over to Newcastle one day when they spotted a hill smack dab in the middle of fields and pastures. It was “love at first sight!”—an answer to problems of living in a small town. They built a big sprawling house on top of that hill and had me. Daddy thought I was going to be a boy and they were going to name me after his college roommate James, but I fooled them so they had to name me Jamie since I turned out to be a girl. My room was on the side of the house next to the doggie yard. Sometimes I got scared at night because Clarence Kunkel told Daddy that Indians used to camp out here and buried their dead on the side of the Hill close to where my room is.

Being born there didn’t make me like the wind whistling ’round the corners of the house or the windows rattling, shaking all day long. Sometimes I’d close myself up in the bathroom and turn on the water in the tub as hard as it would go just so I couldn’t hear the wind blow. But I never thought about wanting to live anywhere else. On still nights the creaking of the windmill put me to sleep. Our barn was a place for make-believe—a playhouse, a hideout, a fortress, a stage for play-acting. The fields and pastures gave me lots of room to run and holler and play cowboys and Indians. I had all the friends I could ever want. Of course, they all had four legs instead of two, but that made them all the better to run with. We had little dogs, big dogs, a few giant dogs, sweet dogs, ornery dogs—all kinds of dogs! Daddy called them the Hill Gang. The membership went up and down all the time. It depended on how many puppies had been born or who decided to move on, or who ran across the highway without looking beforehand, or who was dropped off down the road because some hunter got mad at it for not doing its job. We had lots of those castoffs. I had two special girlfriends, Neva Lou and Eva Joy, but my doggies were my really special friends.

Like all kids I had chores to do, but somehow, they didn’t seem nearly as bad because I had my doggie friends. I managed to play some of the time. Daddy said “a lot.” Mother said that’s all I did—play, that is. The best times were when Daddy and I would sit out on the porch and talk while the sun went down. Mother would be fixing supper and we could smell good things cooking on the stove. We talked about lots of things, but I really liked it when we talked about the dogs we had known, the special ones we loved, and the ones we didn't especially love. We giggled or laughed, remembering some of the dumb things they did. Some had weird stunts they liked to show off. Some were so smart. We wondered what happened to those that moved on. But none of them were "just dogs," as certain people said. We never seemed to run out of dogs to talk about. Sometimes we didn't have to talk at all. Daddy'd give a little cough and pull out his handkerchief and wipe his eyes and I knew he was still talking inside about our dogs. After one of those quiet times he looked over at me like he hadn't seen me before.

"You know, each one of those guys left some kind of mark on you that has helped to make you what you are today. You've learned a lot about life from them."

Well! I sure hoped Ug and Thug didn't make too much of a mark on me, and I hoped there was a big mark from Curley. I worried and worried about those marks, but I needn't have because I turned out all right, though I wonder what Mother means when she says I'm "not out of the oven yet."

One day I decided to sit down on the front porch and start remembering things on paper because I noticed that people kinda forget when they grow older, and I sure didn't want to forget about my friends and some of my not-so-friends. I put all of my remembering down on paper in case when I get to TCU and my head gets too full of learning, or when I get older and forgetful, I can read about my adventures on the Hill and all the dogs I have known, and even Mr. P.

Pobre

Pobre was a pound dog; pound dogs are jailbirds, only it isn't that they've ever done anything really wrong, but they just happened to be born to somebody who didn't want them. Some dogs were there because they had broken a rule, but we never knew about Pobre.

Daddy had to tell me about Pobre's beginnings because they had Pobre before they had me. When he found out I was on the way, he decided a boy needed a dog to grow up with, so he went to the pound and picked out a dog no one else would ever choose. He made two mistakes: I turned out to be a girl and Pobre turned out to be a dog anyone would want. Of course, he didn't start out that way.

Daddy said that when Pobre first came to the Hill, he was skinny, hard-headed, and his black coat looked like worn-out carpet with lots of slashes and tears. His first day on the way home from the pound he threw up on the back seat of the car. First thing when he hopped out of the car on the Hill, he attacked Tiny Tim, our big horse-dog; he marched over to Mother, who was hanging out clothes, looked up at her, raised his leg, and peed on her; then he lifted his nose, took a few sniffs, and headed straight for the dog pan. Without so much as a "May I?" he ducked his head, and in a few short snorts emptied it. Daddy said by that time the other Hill dogs gathered around. They didn't bark; they didn't move a muscle except their eyes as they watched Pobre swagger and strut from dog to dog checking each one out. After his tour of inspection, he hopped up the steps, seated himself on the porch, and declared the back porch his territory and the Hill Gang had better not forget it—and Daddy said they never did.

Those first few weeks Pobre showed everyone how tough he was. He didn't need friends because he could take care of himself. But all of that high and mighty attitude changed, Daddy said, overnight. He woke up to crashing and clanging and thumping and moaning out on the back steps. When he ran to the door and switched on the light, there was a proud, stuck-up Pobre with his head stuck inside a big pickle jar. He had managed to break out the bottom, but he couldn't get rid of the rim and about six inches of jagged glass around his head. Daddy said he broke the rim, and Pobre, almost at the same moment, changed from rough and tough ex-jailbird to a warm and loving friend. But he said that probably my arrival also had something to do with his new "philosophy of life." I never really understood what "philosophy of life" meant until I got a few spankings and Daddy would always say I needed to

change my "philosophy of life" like Pobre did.

So, the Pobre I knew never looked for fights or trouble. Daddy would laugh and say that Pobre was a lover, not a fighter. Oh, he'd raise his hackles and snarl and look fierce, if he thought it was necessary. What he really liked to do, though, was sit at the top of the steps and look out over the countryside to see what was happening in the world—not that he was particularly anxious to do anything about whatever happened to be happening. I always thought he was trying to make up for his wild gangster ways by showing us how law abiding and peace loving he could be. Every so often a grass snake might slither across my path and I'd scream, so Pobre would attack and bring back the body just to show me he had done his duty, but he wasn't happy about the chore.

• • • • • • • •

One summer morning sounds on top of the house woke me up. There were thumps and squeaks and chatter as millions of bodies seemed to swish and scurry in all directions on our roof. I ran into the kitchen just as Daddy came through the back door. He slammed it so hard the dishes rattled on the shelves. He said rats and mice were everywhere and that he'd never seen anything like it. I ran to the window and looked out on our hill full of gray things darting across the yard every which way, shinnying up walls, jumping off the roof, running along the barbed wire on the fence. Our hill looked like an ant hill—only the ants were rats.

That was the beginning day of the plague! I wouldn't go outside that day at all or any days after that, unless Daddy gave me that certain look that meant something worse than rat plague was about to happen if I didn't get moving on my outside chores. Most of the days I stayed inside emptying mouse traps. When the house would get quiet at night the traps sounded like popcorn popping everywhere.

Sometimes if I didn't get the door fast enough a rat would scoot in between my feet. They knocked over candleholders, chewed the glue off of our *National Geographics*, gnawed ivy, and even tore open my bubble gum wrappers and stole my bubble gum! Daddy had to put wire mesh over the chimney to keep them from scooting down through the fireplace. They nested in the motor of the Chevy pickup; they took over the barn, and we couldn't get away from the sounds of their squeals and clicking and pitter-pattering of millions of claws. One night Daddy drove the pickup down to a field and we sat there and watched as armies of mice moved in front of the headlights like gray waves, cleaning out the wheat stubble right down to the ground.

Like Daddy, Pobre must have decided enough was enough. Just like Superman, he left his perch on the porch, shook himself from nose to tail, and right before our eyes changed from peace to war. He raised his hackles, bared his teeth, and attacked. He darted in and out of bushes and flower beds, rooted up boards and rocks, and shot around that yard like a bullet bouncing off of walls and rocks and fence posts. He'd clamp his teeth around the rat's neck, lift the squirming squealing gray body off the ground and shake it and shake it, the tail snapping and whipping till it was dead. Then he'd toss that one over his shoulder and go right on to the next. Daddy let him sleep in the house at night just so he could get a little rest, but every time a mouse trap went off he'd lift his head, perk up his ears, and growl real low. Then I guess he'd remember that he was in the house and go back to sleep. The next day it started all over again. Pobre was the mean, tough fighter he had been when he was a jailbird in the pound. He was a "born-again thug" my daddy said.

The rats and mice stayed all summer. But one morning I woke up—something was different. The windmill was creaking, the chickens were cackling, and there was the usual barnyard clatter. But except for the wind barely moving in the tree branches, everything was still. I ran into the kitchen, looked out into the yard—nothing moving! Not even Pobre! He was back on his perch on the porch, scanning the Hill, but there was nothing to chase. Not a rat or mouse anywhere! Daddy came into the kitchen, sat down at the table shaking his head and said he guessed he'd seen everything now.

"It's like someone or something sounded a signal—rats and mice are gone—just up and gone!" Pobre was very still; his ears were perked and his nose was up; he was listening, looking, listening, and waiting, and waiting.

Miss Petty, my teacher at Olney Elementary, talked about how the Indians used to look out across the prairie, listening, waiting, and watching for the buffalo to come back, but they never did. That's what Pobre did. He sat on the porch, day after day, looking out over the yard, past the barn, listening, waiting, and watching for the rats and mice to come back. But they never did.

J. D. 2

Chickens are selfish and mean—always trying to be first—pecking and fussing at their best friends just to get as close to the feed as they can. You can't walk without stepping in their mess. I never did like feeding those nasty chickens! I was sure glad when J. D. came along wanting to know if Daddy had any work to do. So Daddy took him on. Mother brought out some cold biscuits left over from breakfast and some bologna and gravy. He sat on the back steps and dunked biscuits and smacked and licked till there wasn't anything left. He lived in a little room behind the smokehouse. There was a cot, a wood cook stove, a rickety old rocker, and a rag rug. He liked feeding all the chickens and didn't seem to mind their fidgeting and fussing. In fact, he kinda cackled like they did when he called them. His fingers looked like spider legs scooping up the feed and flinging it out—scooping and scattering and cackling and pecking and fussing. He didn't pay any attention to all that nasty chicken mess.

J. D. was black, but not really; he was more of a light chocolate brown except for big yellow teeth and big yellow eyes. His head hung down between his shoulders. His faded shirt and pants fluttered and his big old feet flapped when he walked. The chickens got more talk from J. D. than we ever did.

One morning while he was feeding them, he just stopped and stood real still, listened, then turned and looked down the road. I couldn't hear anything but J. D. did! Sure enough, in a few seconds a dog came over the lip of our hill and spotted J. D. He went through the gate and stood there wagging his tail and grinning like they were long lost friends. The chickens clucked and clattered but they got out of his way. There they were, standing in the middle of the chicken yard—almost twins. That dog was the same light chocolate reddish brown that J. D. was. He even had yellow eyes and long yellow teeth and his hide stretched over his bones just like J. D. From that day on, I never saw one without the other being close by. So I named him J. D. 2—say it real fast and it sounds okay—"Jadeytoo."

J. D. never got excited about anything: J. D. 2 didn't either, except about food. He'd plow into his dog pan with his floppy jaws, slurping the dried food like it was mush—smacking and sucking sounds like you never heard—looking up every so often as if to say "This is so-o good!" then dipping right down to slurp some more. Other than meal time, J. D. 2 was always trotting right behind J. D., taking every step he did. J. D. acted like he didn't care, but I know he did. J. D. 2 slept with him and I'd hear them talking to each other. I was glad J. D. had somebody to talk to besides those chickens! Lots of times they got tired of J. D. 2 getting in their way at meal time and they'd all tear into him. He'd get between J. D.'s legs and stare them down.

I wondered if J. D. noticed that J. D. 2 wasn't real brave. He'd watch a snake slither by him without so much as a growl, and when coyotes yelled at night he'd just roll his eyes at J. D. to make sure he was still close by, recross his legs, and play like he was sleepy.

J. D. got so sick that Daddy took him to the doctor. Several days later J. D. told Daddy he wanted to go back home. Home was somewhere in East Texas. He said he didn't believe he'd be coming back, but if Daddy'd take him to the bus station, he'd be "much obliged." The morning he left he fed the chickens like he always did; then he squatted down and rubbed J. D. 2 behind the ears, telling him to take care of himself. He crawled into the pickup with Daddy. J. D. 2 watched them go down the Hill, turn on to the old Throckmorton highway to town, and disappear. He sort of wagged his tail, heaved a big sigh, sniffed a few spots, then headed down the road to the highway. The last time I saw him he was trotting through the bar ditch, headed west with his tail up and his nose in to the air, ready for whatever scents were in the wind.

Posse

The minute I saw her I knew she was what I'd been waiting for, and waiting for a long time! She wagged her tail for us, squirming around making funny little noises. Her coat was soft fuzzy gray and white. Her paws were awfully big for a puppy; Daddy said that was a sign she'd grow up to be a big dog. She looked like she was wearing a mask—black all around light blue eyes. Daddy paid the man some money. He put her into my arms. I hugged her; she grunted and squealed, snuggled her nose under my arm, and I knew she was all mine.

On the way home I looked at her the whole time, trying to think of the perfect name for her. The black mask made me think of the Lone Ranger. Maybe that was it—Lone Ranger. I couldn't call a girl Lone Ranger. Robbers? Posses? That was it! I'd call her Posse.

Posse was a husky. Huskies like the cold—like in Alaska. But we lived in West Texas, where it gets so hot the asphalt bubbles in the summertime. I guess that's why Posse never had a thick coat of fur. She certainly didn't look like the pictures I'd seen of huskies pulling sleds up at the North Pole. In fact, she was sort of bald in spots and her coat got slicker instead of fluffier. Since she didn't have polar bears to chase or chunks of ice to float on, she swam in tanks to keep cool, or she'd gather up the other dogs on the Hill to chase cattle. Maybe I should have called her something else—Annie, or Tammy, or somebody nice so maybe she'd act nicer. I believe dogs kinda act like their names sometimes. But it was too late to change anything. She was hardheaded and did what she wanted to do when SHE wanted to do it! Oh she'd mind me if I had a goodie for her or if I got real mad and hollered "POSSSSEEEE!"

The farmers and ranchers all knew her and knew who to call when Posse and her friends chased their cattle. When Daddy'd hang up the phone after one of those calls, he'd grab her by the neck and run her into the dog yard just fussin' and threatenin' all kinds of bad things would happen to her if she didn't "straighten out" and behave herself. Posse didn't bark like a dog; she'd start off with a low moan that seemed to come from way down, and by the time it got out it was more like croaking and gargling at the same time. After a whole night of that, Daddy would stomp out the next morning and tell her he'd let her out if she'd act right. She wouldn't even slow down as she ran past him through the gate—never said thank you or anything—just left him standing there with his hands on his hips shaking his head.

One evening Posse didn't show up for supper. I checked her pan before I went to bed but she had not come home even to eat. That night and lots of nights after, whenever I'd wake up, I'd go to the balcony and call and call, as loud as I could, "Pos-s-s-ee . . . Pos-s-s-ee!" She should have heard it miles away because everything was so still and quiet. I looked as hard as I could through the shadows of the mesquites and the streaks of moonlight for something to move. Nothing. Some farmer or rancher had shot her, and I'd never see her again.

Late one night something woke me up. Sounds like things

shuffling around on the porch—throaty soft cries that could only belong to Posse! I threw back the covers and dashed for the light switch, but Daddy had beaten me to it. There stood Posse! She was making her funny sounds and swishing her tail and squirming and smiling. I hugged her and hugged her. She licked my face.

"Oh, Posse! Where have you been? What have you been doing? Why have you stayed gone so long? Why didn't you come when I called you?"

She kept licking and nuzzling and then . . . I saw HIM! Standing there, looking at us was the biggest, most beautiful black dog I had ever seen! His coat was thick long fur that looked like a robe—the royal robe of the Black Knight! He waved his tail like it was a banner, the only sign that he wasn't a statue. All of a sudden Posse stopped her greetings, her ears stood up, and she looked straight into my eyes as if to tell me she still loved me, but then she looked at him and by some silent signal they turned and disappeared into the darkness, as if they had never been there at all. I didn't call her back. I knew she wouldn't come.

Posse came home not long after that night. She dragged herself to the dog pan. Her tail was hanging low. She didn't raise her head and her ears were flat. Even my hugging her didn't perk her up. She ate a few bites. Then she crawled into her house and slept. She slept all of that day. It felt so good to have her home. I'd just go by her house and look at her asleep. She seemed to be smiling. Sometimes she'd jerk her paws and make small sounds. She was dreaming of her Black Knight. For a long time after she came back, late at night, she'd cry her funny cry. Way, way off I could hear the barks of dogs running across the prairie; the sounds would finally fade away; then Posse would duck her head, wag her tail, and crawl back into her house.

I wondered why she didn't run off to join him.

One morning I knew why.

There were lots of little puppy sounds coming from her house, and when I peeked inside, I could just barely see lots of little shining slick balls of fur—some gray and white, some all black.

ROTARY
Eat

May-ree

Most of the ranchers and farmers around us leased their fields and pastures during bird season to hunters from Olney. Early in the morning and late in the afternoon we could hear the pop-pop of guns all over the countryside. The hunters started shooting doves in September and quail in December, and they were real picky about their dogs. Daddy said some of them spent hundreds of dollars for just one. The only fun the dogs ever had was during bird season because the rest of the time they were locked up in small pens. If the dog didn't do his hunting job right, lots of times the hunter would just dump him and go off and leave him in some pasture and never tell him he was going or why. Several of those orphans wound up on the Hill, hungry and scared and no place to go.

May-ree wandered up the Hill one October afternoon. She was a freckled brown and white bird dog with long limp ears, a tongue that hung almost to the ground, and big feet. Her ribs stuck out and her sides caved in. I put some food in a pan and took her out to the barn, introduced her to the Hill Gang, fluffed up some hay and told her she was welcome here.

No matter how dirty dogs might be when they found us on the Hill, they'd soon get themselves all cleaned up, doing whatever it is that dogs do to look nice. May-ree looked just as dirty the next morning as she had the night before; a week later, the same. It wasn't that she was covered with mud or anything like that. It didn't feel good to pet her—the white hair was gray, the brown was a rusty-dusty sort of color. Her breath was like stagnant water—well really she smelled so awful all over it was hard to tell where it was coming from in particular. The Hill Gang tried to be nice, but they really didn't want to have anything to do with her. They'd decide to explore a pasture and take off. She'd lope, ears flopping, trying to catch up with them. She was the last one out and the last one in. Daddy or I would stop to pet her and she'd roll on her back, wallow around, and spread her legs out. Daddy'd fuss at her and tell her to "stand tall" and be proud. I guess she didn't think she had anything to be proud about. As far as I could see, she didn't, but I wasn't going to tell her that.

Every year at rodeo time there was a big parade down Main Street the opening day. All the clubs in Olney made floats. Since Daddy was a member of the Rotary Club, he had to help. He said they were going to do what he called a Spudnut, since the Russians had sent one into space with a dog inside it, and he was in charge of getting the dog because everybody knew we had lots of dogs. I didn't know what a Spudnut was, but I knew this was May-ree's chance to get lots of attention and maybe this would make her "stand tall" and be proud. I begged him to choose May-ree, so he did.

The morning before the parade I took May-ree down to the tank for a bath. Actually, she didn't mind at all. She stood in the shallow water real still and let me soap and scrub her. When I finished, she stepped out of the water like she didn't want to splash and mess her hairdo. Her tail wagged all the way back to the house. Daddy opened the pickup door for her, took off his hat and bowed like in the movies; she hopped in and seated herself like she was Elizabeth Taylor. Down the Hill they went in a puff of dust. Mighta been dust, but my eyes were all watery as I watched them turn on to the highway—May-ree sitting as tall as Daddy in the front seat of the pickup.

When the Rotary float came down the street, there was the Spudnut! It looked like strips of wood bent into circles wrapped in Reynolds Wrap, making a big ball of circles, and sitting in the middle was May-ree. They had put a collar on her and attached a leash, just in case, I guess. She looked so scared she couldn't move anyhow. All along the street people clapped and pointed and laughed when they saw the Rotary float and May-ree perched inside the Spudnut. When May-ree came home, the first thing she did was run to the barn to tell the Hill Gang about her adventure. All of a sudden, they had things to do out in the pasture and ran out leaving May-ree with no one to wag her tail to. She threw her head back, squared her shoulders, and ran till she caught up with the pack. When they came back, she wasn't the first one in, but she wasn't the last one either.

Wookie

Since her mother was a junkyard dog, Wookie was part of lots of things, but mostly she was German shepherd. Her life began in a place where plumbers threw broken toilets and rusty pipes, but we saved her from following in her mother's footsteps when we took her out to the Hill. I never knew why she was invited to live with us; usually all of our dogs invited themselves, or someone would dump an unwanted friend near our place, knowing it would find its way to our house and would be taken care of. Because we did have so many castoffs, Daddy said we just couldn't afford to have all of them "fixed." Most of the time Mother Nature took pity on us because we didn't have that many problems with mothers and puppies—except for Wookie.

Wookie was always "expecting." When she had puppies, she had them by the dozen. Sometimes she'd have three batches in a year's time. Daddy said she was a "born" mother who just liked having babies. Wookie's romances were hard to understand. Probably this was because her boyfriends didn't have very good smellers. Wookie could be below the Hill, out of sight, and if the wind was from her direction you'd think there was a pile of dirty tennis shoes down there. She was a sweet dog and I loved her, but it was hard to hug her neck and hold my nose at the same time. She didn't know she smelled like BO. Lots of times neighbors would drop by and visit Daddy. They'd stand out in the yard and talk and talk; then the neighbor's nose would begin to twitch and sniff until he couldn't keep his mind on what he was saying and he'd finally have to ask Daddy if something was dead. Daddy'd just nod his head toward Wookie. Her fur was so thick she never got cold when it was five below, and I guess it protected her from the heat too because even when the thermometer stayed over a hundred for days at a time, she didn't lose a hair. Year after year it just got thicker—"mellowing" Daddy called it. Well, one summer Daddy said enough was enough! He marched out of the barn and came back waving the sheep shears in hand and heading in on Wookie with a wild look in his eye. Wookie was wagging her tail, expecting loving and petting, and had stretched out on the ground to enjoy it. Daddy squatted down, flipped on the shears and started stripping poor Wookie. She was so shocked she couldn't or wouldn't move, but her eyes bugged out and rolled around to look at him in terror. Daddy was shearing and snorting and gagging and flinging hunks of hair all around himself and Wookie. Fuzz was swirling everywhere—into Daddy's nose, his mouth, sticking on his sweaty neck, and when he stopped, Wookie was NAKED! For a second she didn't move, then she hopped up and as if to cover herself, she tucked her tail between her legs and ran into the barn and stayed there. I'd take food out to her and I guess she'd come out after dark because I'd never see her. The pan was always empty the next morning. That year she had only one batch of puppies. Finally, her coat grew back, but she always stayed away from Daddy, and if he made any quick movements around her she ran for cover.

All of the dogs of the Hill depended on Wookie to tell them what to do and what not to do. She was like a grandmother to them. She stayed close to the house. They would roam the pastures and fields having all kinds of adventures. During the hot part of the day they'd gather in the shade behind the barn, where the trough kept the ground cool and damp, and tell her about all the exciting things that had happened since their last visit. She depended on their adventures instead of having any of her own.

The last year of her life, her back leg got stiff and she had trouble getting up and lying down. Finally, she quit moving at all except for a flutter of the tail if somebody came by. One Saturday morning Daddy and I went into town to get some groceries. On the way home, we passed a dog walking along the shoulder of the road. Daddy put the brakes on. He backed up and whistled but the dog wouldn't come to him. He opened a package of chicken and started throwing out skin and neck and giblets all along the way home until we turned to go up our road. The dog stopped and wouldn't go past the gate. By that time Daddy had run out of chicken. After we took the groceries to the house, I ran back to the lip of the Hill to see if the dog had decided to come up the road. It was still standing at the gate wondering what to do, then it turned away and disappeared in the weeds of the bar ditch. But Wookie! Wookie had pulled herself up and was staggering to the edge of the Hill. Dragging that leg behind her, she stumped down the road, slanting and swaying and barely swishing her tail like it was her rudder. She ducked her head down and made it to the front gate and disappeared in the weeds, too. Pretty soon Wookie came back on to the highway leading that bedraggled dog. She waddled up the Hill; the dog trotted behind her. They headed into the yard but the dog stopped at the fence. Wookie turned around, nodded for it to come on, then went over to her place and lay down. The dog sat next to her, not knowing what to do. But she was through; she had done her duty: the new dog on the Hill was on its own now.

Wookie passed on that afternoon.

Tootie & Katy

When we topped a hill and swooped down to the tank, we probably looked like an army of dogs, except, of course, Daddy and I stood out a little taller. We never went walking without the whole Hill Gang. Daddy believed in being fair to everyone—if one was invited, they all came; if one got a bone, there had to be enough for everyone. Being fair didn't always work because all the Hill Gang couldn't snuggle under the covers with me on those blue norther nights—only Tootie and Katy were invited.

When the wind whistled under the door, they'd sit on the floor and let their teeth chatter and their shoulders shiver and beg with their great big black eyes for an invitation to sleep on the bed that night. Of course, they were never turned down. But being house dogs had its drawbacks. Tootie and

Katy were schnauzers and "family," and it didn't sound right to call them dogs. I'd forget they were dogs until they'd pull some dog stunt, like rolling in the hide of some long dead rabbit and crawling up in bed with me!

Since they had house privileges, they had to endure tick inspection every time they were petted, and it meant frequent trips to the beauty shop (the other dogs were never told where the little pink and yellow ribbons Tootie and Katy wore every other Saturday came from). It seemed like every trip to the beauty parlor, Daddy griped a little louder and longer until finally one Saturday after paying their bill, he dumped them into the back seat, gripped the steering wheel, licked his upper lip, and declared this was the last trip to Patty's Petite Parlor for Tootie and Katy.

"Enough's enough!" he growled.

Both of them cut their eyes at him and wagged their tail stubs and said they had had enough, too.

• • • • • • • •

Each morning they'd stick their whiskers in my face to tell me it was time to get up, and every day the whiskers got stiffer and smellier. I thought I was the only one suffering from their BO until one morning Daddy was standing in my door with a bar of soap and two big towels. I was going to be their new beauty operator. They knew it was the beginning of a bad day and I had the same feeling. Daddy's look cut off any argument I might have thought up. Tootie and Katie didn't argue either.

They threw back the covers and shot under the bed. After several trips around the room, we managed to capture both of them. With their ears laid back, their tails tucked down, and their black eyes bulging, I hauled them into the bathroom, barricaded the door, and the war was on!

Katy was first to go in the water. She stiffened her legs and nothing would bend. I pulled her hind leg like they do the calves at branding time, only she slipped and went under. Tootie looked at what was happening to Katy and hid behind the commode. How could they think I'd ever do anything bad to THEM! I pushed one end down and the other would come up. They flopped and waved their arms and stretched their necks and bugged their eyes. They slung water on the floor, and suds ran down the mirror on the medicine cabinet. Dog hair was sticking to my face and in my mouth, and we were sliding and sloshing against the walls and into the pipes under the sink, until finally I just said, "Okay, enough's enough! All right for you!"

I threw down the towels and left them soapy and shaking on the bathroom floor. If they didn't care, I wouldn't either and they could just stink all the way to Newcastle, but I was finished!

Whatever they went through that morning wasn't anything compared to what was going to happen to them later. Daddy heard about a place where dogs could be clipped, washed, and dried at about half the cost of Patty's Petite Parlor. Of course, we had to do the work. So the four of us went to the dog washateria. Funny how they knew to start shaking, even when they hadn't been told anything about anything.

We put Tootie in the drying room, while Katy went first. Katy got stiff-legged again and wouldn't bend anything, but the collar around her neck kept her from jumping off of the table. So Daddy turned on the clippers and away he went. He started up the middle of her back while I talked to her and rubbed her behind the ears. She didn't want to listen to anything I had to say, and she sure didn't want her ears rubbed. Daddy snarled, curled his lips, squinted his eyes, and attacked poor Katy. He hopped around waving those shears, then running those clippers up and down and around like he was pushing a lawnmower, and when he stopped there stood poor Katy looking like a plowed cornfield. He grabbed the toenail clippers to trim her claws. When she bellowed, he dropped that paw and started on the other. The next cry brought the owner to Katy's rescue.

She told Daddy he'd better just take those dogs to the vet to get their nails cut because a vet knew how to do it right. Both of Katy's feet were bleeding and she was hysterical. Daddy tried to tell her he was sorry, but she wouldn't listen. Tootie was watching from the drying room, and when Daddy reached down to pick her up she let out a long, low growl, hunkered down, then shot between his legs and hid behind the wash rack. Daddy crawled around on his hands and knees trying to tell Tootie everything was going to be all right—just come on out—and finally, she did. He picked her up, petted her and plunked her down on the table.

Tootie bucked like a wild horse. The scissors slipped and her ear got it! We didn't think it was a bad cut, but she wouldn't let us see. She kept swinging her head around, splattering Daddy's shirt with polka dots of blood. Suddenly he stopped, very slowly laid the scissors on the tray, unplugged the clippers, wiped his forehead on his sleeve, and between clinched teeth declared, "Enough's enough!"

Katy and Tootie stopped squirming, looked at each other, and even managed a halfway wag. He took Tootie and paid the lady. I carried Katy. As we headed for the car, their ears perked up, their tails went into full wags. By the time we piled into the car and were halfway down the block, they were squirming with joy.

They didn't notice that Daddy had turned down the street to Patty's Petite Parlor.

Sam

The Trophy Yard was outside the dog fence and all the goodies the dogs found on their adventures were brought there to show and tell about or to munch and crunch. The usual trophies were snakes or rabbits, sometimes a possum or even the skull of a long-dead cow—just what could be found in the fields or pastures around the Hill. Since there were a lot of dogs in the Hill Gang at that time, the Trophy Yard looked like a rotten meat market some mornings. Seemed like each dog tried to outdo the others by dragging in the most or the smelliest victims. Daddy said there was no telling what they'd drag in next, so he checked it out, "just in case," every day. One morning he found a leather work glove, the next day the other one showed up—every day something different—a "gimme" cap, a shoe, the other shoe, and curious things that certainly didn't grow in any field or pasture around our hill. As the days passed, the lot piled up—work boots, goggles, knee pads, pink and white towels, and even a pair of jeans. Daddy kinda jumped every time the phone rang.

Because some of the stolen stuff was too big for any of the little dogs to carry, he decided it had to be one of the big ones—that meant Tiny Tim or Baby or Caleb or Sam. Tiny Tim had been living with us about three years, and he wasn't ever interested in anything but something to eat. Daddy thought Baby was "too mature and dignified" to steal anything. Caleb or Sam had to be guilty since they were the newest dogs in the gang.

Daddy worried that the dogs might not respect cats, so cats were never invited to stay on the Hill. On a still night, every once in a while, we'd hear cats tearing into each other, screeching and yowling, but they didn't come around our place. That's why finding that first kitten in the Trophy Yard was a real surprise. It looked like it had been drowned. The next day another one showed up, and with the third little body Daddy muttered, "Enough's enough!"

He stalked into the house and came back carrying his binoculars. He said we were going to have an "intelligence operation." That scared me, for I knew Daddy didn't know how to cut Katy's toenails, let alone operate on dogs, but he explained we would spy on the Hill Gang until we found out who was being so bad. Anytime the big ones went on their meanderings, I could climb the ladder to the smokehouse roof and watch where they went and what they were doing with his binoculars. I could "survey" the countryside and give him my reports at supper. Well, I sure liked that! I could see Par Herring hanging out clothes two miles away and Ben Stowe smoking a cigarette on his tractor, and I could tell the colors of the cows standing in the tanks way over on the Krueger place. I watched a roadrunner flapping through the field with a mouse in its beak. I tried to watch bull bats diving, but they went too fast and I couldn't keep up with them. There wasn't much going on that I couldn't see with Daddy's binoculars.

When the big dogs headed out for the day's adventures, I waited till they were out of sight, then I climbed the ladder to my post on the smokehouse, looked through the binoculars, and spied on them just like in the movies. They trotted along, each one finding something different to sniff at. One would scare out a rabbit, and they'd all tear out after it until it disappeared. Then they'd dance around barking and yapping, get tired of that and head off for something else. Lots of the times they went Indian style along their paths. That's when I discovered that Sam wasn't with them anymore. Where was Sam?

It was hard to see the whole countryside through those two holes in the binoculars. I looked up and down and sideways and back and forth and back and forth. Where did he go? Daddy was going to be mad at both of us if I didn't get him located. After a long time of looking I decided to see what Ben Stowe was doing on his tractor. Nothing, just bumping along thinking about things, it looked like. I wondered if the cows were still standing in the tank getting cool.

They hadn't moved, but there was Sam standing in there with them, only he was moving! Up and down, up and down, bobbing his head like it was on some kind of spring and he had something in his mouth that was getting the bobbing—and I knew what it was!

The next morning, cat number four was out in the Trophy Yard. Sam had snuck it in during the night and there it lay for everyone to see! That did it! Daddy said since Sam didn't know how to act, he'd have to pay the price. He marched Sam to the yard where the dipping pen was, shoved him in and latched the gate. Sam stayed in jail a week.

When Daddy let him out he talked to him about behaving and doing right. I don't think Sam was mad at us, but he didn't come over to thank us before he took off. He was sure glad to get out of the pen so he could run and explore and do things with the gang again. With a yip and a bark he hightailed it over the Hill and disappeared in the mesquites.

• • • • • • • •

Daddy went into town one stormy morning, not long after Sam was freed, to drink coffee with his friends. When I heard him come up the Hill and slam on the brakes and the back door about the same time, I knew there was more than one storm and it was coming down the hall.

"Clay Williams has lost all of his rabbits! The cages were all torn open and the rabbits pulled out and killed! Just killed and thrown on the ground. Didn't even bother to eat them—just killed for the meanness of it! He says it was one of our dogs, and we know who he means, don't we?"

Daddy said he paid Clay $132 for the rabbits and that Clay'd let him know how much it cost to build back the pen. Well, that was the end of Sam's free roaming days. Daddy put him in the dipping pen where he lived except at dipping time. Then he'd get a parole to the dog yard till all the sheep had been done. When the dipping was over, he was locked up again, just like they do in prisons.

WOW

White on White doesn't sound colorful for a dog's name, but put it into initials and it sounds more exciting—like WOW! Well, that was Daddy's name for the newest member of the Hill Gang. Daddy's names for dogs were kinda dumb. But WOW it was. At least we didn't have to holler, "Here, White on White!" when we called him.

WOW wandered into the pecan orchard when Daddy was standing in the bed of the pickup harvesting the new crop of pecans. If we didn't get to the pecans before they fell out of the hulls, we didn't get any because as soon as they hit the ground the rats had their own harvest, and we were without pecans for the next year. Daddy was shaking a limb, trying to get a cluster to fall, when he said he heard a "Hhh-Ruumphh." He looked down and saw a saucy little dog standing with his legs spread out and his tail curled over his back. With big brown eyes bugging out at him it was like he was saying, "Here I am and aren't you lucky to have me here inviting myself to this auspicious occasion because I'm a pretty auspicious guy." Daddy laughed and said he guessed that the white-on-white dog thought his presence made the occasion auspicious because there's certainly nothing auspicious about picking pecans in the bed of a pickup. That was a day to remember because not only did we meet WOW for the first time, but that's when I learned what "auspicious" meant, too. Somehow, from that time on those two words always seemed to run together—WOW-AUSPICIOUS-WOW.

Usually Daddy let me have all the dogs on the Hill, but WOW became his dog. Actually, WOW looked like he was glued to Daddy's right heel. His steps were as big as Daddy's. Sometimes he'd prance ahead of him, turn around and say, "This is the way to go, Dummy. How'd you ever manage before I came along?" Then he'd strut ahead as if he'd been there a dozen times before when really he hadn't. He was such a "know-it-all."

Naturally, some of the older dogs got tired of WOW's bragging and cockiness. Ug and Thug, Dubie's two sons, snarled and growled at WOW every time they thought no one was looking. WOW never missed a chance to show them how "auspicious" he was. He would bare his teeth, lay his ears flat, and growl and snarl right back at them, always keeping his eyes rolled at Daddy just to make sure Daddy could see how brave and tough he could be. Besides that, I think he felt safer knowing that help wasn't far away, just in case. WOW would never admit that though. Even if he had just been fed, sometimes he'd march over, take a lump of food out of their bowls, waller and crunch it around in his mouth, gulp, waggle his curled up tail in their faces and swagger off like John Wayne. His nose was so high in the air he didn't see those two black dogs bare their fangs and slowly whip their tails back and forth like knife blades—back and forth, back and forth.

Daddy talked to WOW about being so cocky and told him those two guys were gonna get even with him some day if he didn't watch out. WOW would always grin, lick his chops, and talk about other things more important.

Daddy never left home without putting WOW in the dog yard and making sure the gate was locked. The two brothers would bring up all kinds of little animals, sometimes dead, sometimes dying, toss them around on the grass outside the fence, play with them a while, and then eat them right in front of WOW. WOW went crazy, barking, hollering, climbing, and clawing, trying to get over the fence. He forgot all about being cool or cocky—or auspicious. All he could think about was getting out of that dog yard.

We went to Boyd to spend the day with Grandmother and didn't head for home until after dark. I was sound asleep in the back seat when I heard Daddy groan, "Oooh-WOW! WOW-IE!" and slam on the brakes so hard I landed in the floor. He threw open the door and started running. The headlights shone on a still white form just outside the fence of the dog yard. Daddy picked up WOW. He held him and rocked back and forth saying over and over "WOW—oh WOW-ie . . ." but WOW didn't move.

CHEVROLET
"Gone Fishing"
D 99
Texas

Dubie

Do you remember the dog Wookie brought up to the house the day she died? That dog decided she would stay with us. Daddy named this one, too. He called her Dubie, short for Dubious, because he said he wasn't sure whether or not she really was a dog. Her hide looked like it was sort of draped between tent poles except when she gorged herself; then her stomach swelled out like a burlap bag of peanuts. Her feet were as big as mine. One ear stood up and the other just flopped around. Someone must have taken a butcher knife to her tail because it looked like it had been hacked off, and hair never did grow over the end of it like it did when other dogs had their tails cut. She took Wookie's place in the puppy business except her puppies were so ugly we had a hard time giving them away.

Two of her kids we had to keep, two boys, and we named them Ug and Thug. Terrible, I know, to give them such awful names, particularly when you think about how dogs kinda act like their names. Maybe if we'd named them Black Beauty and Black Flash or something like that, things would have been different. Every time I'd think I was going to call them something nicer, Ug or Thug would just come out.

Ug and Thug followed their momma like two black shadows. Dubie stopped hanging her head all the time, and she seemed to prance when she walked. She sat looking out of her doghouse like it was her castle—all the lands around were hers to rule. She told Ug and Thug what to do and when to do it. Oh they would snarl and show their fangs, but they did mind her. It didn't seem to bother her that they were almost twice as big as she was. Maybe she couldn't see what monsters they were. Daddy warned me to stay out of their way and not to cross them. He was always watching WOW, and again and again told him to leave those guys alone.

Late at night Dubie and Ug and Thug would go hunting. We could hear them barking and hollering way over in some field or pasture when they had some poor animal cornered. The next morning a half-eaten rabbit or punctured rattlesnake would lie sprawled out on the ground in front of the dog-yard fence, which made WOW go crazy on the other side. Ug and Thug would smirk at each other and then start tearing and gnawing on their kill.

The Sunday night that we found WOW dead in the driveway, we found the hide and hair of a rabbit, too. Ug and Thug had teased WOW until he couldn't stand it any longer. Somehow he climbed up the fence and over it to get to the carcass. That's what they had been waiting for!

Daddy picked WOW up and carried him into the garage and laid him on some feed sacks. He went into the house and came back carrying his shotgun. He slowly walked over to the pickup, opened the door, placed the gun in its rack, and called Dubie to come. She trotted over, wagged her stumpy tail, and hopped into the cab. She was always so glad to have some attention paid to her. In a very calm voice, Daddy invited Thug and Ug to get in with their momma. They looked at each other and decided they wouldn't, but Dubie sent the message that they had better get up there with her or else. So they slunk in beside her. Daddy opened the door on the driver's side and let Dubie out. He crawled in, fired up the motor, turned on the lights, and disappeared over the lip of the Hill. I watched the taillights as long as I could. They went down the highway, turned off on the dirt road about half a mile from the house, heading north, and then into blackness.

When Daddy came back, I had been in bed trying to go to sleep for a long time. I didn't get up, but I could hear him out in the garage talking to poor WOW. I didn't think daddies ever cried, but I knew my daddy was crying. I don't think anybody got much sleep that night. Lights kept going off and on all over the house, and every once in a while the screen door would slam.

• • • • • • • •

Fog would usually fill the fields and pasture in the

early mornings, but it never got up the Hill to the house. The next morning we couldn't see the barns or the telephone poles or the end of the fence in the dog yard. It was like a big soft gray blanket was covering our house and the whole world, as if the sun didn't want to shine on the day we had to bury WOW. The fog seemed to creep into the house, too; Daddy was sitting at the table in the kitchen looking into a cup of cold coffee when I came in for breakfast. He pushed back his chair, picked up his hat, and said he was going to take care of WOW. I said I wanted to help so I ran to the closet and got a nice pillowcase and we went out to the pile of burlap bags. Daddy gently picked up WOW and placed him in the pillowcase. He was laying him into the bed of the pickup when we heard a "rr-uuu-rr-aa-a-uu-ww"—deep and long and hurting.

Coming through the mist around the corner was Ug. The fog was so thick it was like he didn't have any legs but he just seemed to wobble and sway. Trying to wag his tail, he almost seemed to be swimming right toward us. Then I saw his face. There was a big bloody hole on the side of his head under his ear. His eyes seemed to roll like slow-moving marbles. He just kept moaning and coming right at us. Daddy and I stood there. I couldn't move and I guess he couldn't either; then he grabbed me by the shoulders and guided me into the cab of the pickup, slammed the door, and turned to face Ug. He circled around him and then I couldn't see him anymore. I heard the screen door bang, a few seconds another bang, and Daddy came back through the fog towards Ug. Like in slow motion, he came up behind him and grabbed a handful of fur and they disappeared into the fog. I was shivering so hard my teeth were shaking. I couldn't see anything no matter how hard I looked. The whole world was gray. I looked at the drops of water on the windshield and waited. After a long, long time I heard a gun shoot. It was far away—once, twice, three times—finally the sounds of footsteps on gravel. Daddy rose up through the fog, crawled into the pickup, started the motor, and we went down the Hill to the dog cemetery to bury WOW.

A. R.

Lots of times I heard Daddy talk about how A. R. was the "all-American boy." Of course, A. R. was no boy because he was as big as Daddy and he had three real boys of his own. Daddy said his high school sweetheart was "Most Beautiful" and he was captain of the football team. When he went to college at A&M he led the troops, and then went into the Air Corps and flew "the big ones." Daddy said A. R. could have led a wagon train or a space flight. He was always dreaming and talking about new frontiers, but for a living, he was a pumper checking out oil leases for people. They drank coffee at the Dairy Queen on rainy mornings and became good friends, so good that Daddy told us to call A. R. if we ever needed somebody in a hurry when he wasn't around.

I slept with Mother while Daddy was away at a meeting in Fort Worth. Thunder rolled and lightning jagged all night so I was glad I didn't have to stay in my bed by myself. Early in the morning a scratching and thumping against the window woke us up. There was just enough light to make out a ball of fur shivering and climbing outside on the window frame. We watched it go along the edge of the window, up, across, and down the other side; then it waddled over the decking to the gate into the dog yard and disappeared. Mother said it was a raccoon, and the dogs would scare it off. But all was quiet—not a bark from anyone. Daddy always warned that wild things didn't come around humans unless they were sick—and usually they were rabid. I ran to my bedroom window and watched it poke around the dog pans and sniff the ground. Then I guess it got tired so it went into the doghouse and didn't come out. Mother decided she'd better call A. R. to come do something about it before the dogs came in from their morning meanderings. He said he'd be right out, for us not to do anything.

Finally through the mist and rain we saw a pickup coming down the highway, turning up the road to the Hill—A. R. at last. Almost before the motor stopped, he threw open the door, grabbed the gun from the rack, slammed the door, and when he came around the front of the pickup, he was ready for battle. By then the doggies who were scattered around the fields and pastures enjoying their early morning adventures were coming in to see what was happening up at the house. We could almost hear their brakes squeal as each one got close enough to see A. R. He looked like John Wayne in "The Green Berets"—brown and green and gray clothes like they wear in the army, pants legs stuffed into big heavy boots, his gimme cap pulled low over one eye, and with both hands holding a gun the size of a cannon.

"He's going to attack the house!" Mother moaned.

"He's going to attack the doggies! Mother, do SOMETHING!"

Well, that whole herd of doggies seemed to melt away, right there in the rain. They slipped behind bushes, they crawled under rocks, and hid under the wheels of A. R.'s pickup. He didn't pay any attention to them or how scared they were. He was beading in on the raccoon. He tiptoed over to the gate, carefully lifted the latch. Crouching down like they do in the movies, he darted from bush to bush to tree trunk until he stopped right in front of the doghouse. Sucking in his breath and without moving his mouth, he gritted, "OKAY, YOU! Come out, OR ELSE!"

Either the rain was making so much noise on the tin roof of the doghouse or he was thinking too hard about blowing that raccoon to pieces, but A. R. didn't hear Mother hollering at him not to shoot, not to shoot! So she grabbed my arm and yanked me away from the window and out of the room. Then she flew out the door and into the rain hollering and screaming for A. R. not to shoot that big gun.

"You'll blow away half the . . ."

KA-BOOM-BOOM-M-M-M!

Like a cannon ball, something blew the doghouse to splinters, tore through my bedroom wall, plowed up the floor, and finally stopped somewhere down under the foundation in the living room. After the smoke and dust settled, the rain stopped, and A. R.'s pickup was gone, the doggies hoped it was safe to come out of the bushes and from under the rocks. Their tails were sagging, their ears were slicked back, and they hunkered down as low as they could, kinda slithering along the ground, hoping nobody'd notice them. The two under A. R.'s pickup must have realized their hidey-hole was a battlefield because we didn't see them till suppertime. We never found hide or hair of the raccoon; our doggies would never be the same—"shell shock" Daddy called it—and I never heard Daddy call A. R. the "all-American boy" again. He had other names for him, but not that one.

Fillene

Aida's name should have been Lolita, Daddy said. I wanted to know why but he'd just grin and say, "because." Aida was mommy to Fillene and lots of others. She acted like she cared about her puppies until weaning time—after that they were on their own. She was through being "mommy." Aida's last litter was about six weeks old when the weather turned so cold their water froze in the pan before all eight puppies could get a good slurp. Even though they slept on top of each other in their house, I guess they decided it was warmer back under the rocks on the edge of the Hill. Maybe that's why they decided to stay there instead of their doghouse. They came running up to the house at meal call, but the rest of the time they enjoyed romping and rolling out of the wind on the side of the Hill.

We started missing one, then two. Because it was so

cold, we really couldn't spend a lot of time crawling around and through the rocks looking for puppies that didn't want to be found. We were going up to Colorado to ski for a week and the Herrings would have to look after everything. I didn't want to go off and leave the missing puppies. Daddy said they would be all right, and we certainly weren't going to cancel our plans because of a pack of puppies, and that was all there was to it!

Daddy wasn't wrong many times, but this time he was. When we drove up the Hill a week later, not a puppy in sight. Aida was perched on her throne; she did bother to raise herself up, fan her tail at us, lift her ears like she knew we were home, but ho-hum, so what. Daddy muttered something about her being a "blue-blooded watchdog all right" and opened the garage door. I ran over to the edge of the Hill, calling, "Puppies! Puppies! We're home. Here, puppy, puppies!" The only sound was the wind clicking the icy weeds together. No puppies.

"Aida! Where are your babies?" I screamed.

Like in slow motion, she stepped down, sniffed a few spots, and then climbed back on her throne "like the Queen of the Nile," Daddy said. Neither one of us found any sign of a single puppy; they had all disappeared. I got down on my hands and knees for one last look in the doghouse. Two little shiny eyes were bulging out at me. Daddy came running and stuck his arm in and finally managed to pull a squealing, growling little puppy out. It quivered and hunched into a tight furry ball. He couldn't stand, and there were dark stiff patches of fur and great big holes in his back. The soft puppy look in his eyes was gone—now he looked like those cornered rats Pobre used to catch. What had happened to him? What had happened to his brothers and sisters? Was he the only one left? Why was he alive if the others were dead? Daddy tried to calm him down, telling him he was safe and we weren't going to hurt him.

Aida sat on her throne watching us with half-closed

eyes. When Daddy picked the puppy up to take in to the house, his mommy was snoring.

I found a box and put a soft blanket in it for a bed and that's where he stayed. I named him Fillene. He didn't bark, he didn't seem hungry, and he didn't want to close his eyes, but sometimes he was so tired he had to. Wherever I went, Fillene went too. One morning he woke me up growling and pulling at the sheet. His stubby tail was standing up and wagging. He was out of his box! Except for his left rear leg, everything seemed to be working okay. At last he was doing what other doggies did, but he was so-o-o spoiled. If the other dogs invited him to play, he would, but if I went into the house he stopped whatever he was doing and trotted right behind me. Daddy said he stayed in his box until he heard the school bus coming, then he'd hop out and be waiting at the door to welcome me home.

• • • • • • • •

By the time Fillene was six months old, he looked like a big black bear. Daddy kept asking him when he was going to lose his baby fur. He slept on the bed with me. That meant one little edge of the bed for me; Fillene sprawled out over the rest.

Spring cleaning took at least a week. Mother attacked the whole house at once—from washing windows, to airing curtains, to waxing floors, to vacuuming upholstery, to putting new carpet in the guest bedroom. Daddy had done a little spring cleaning of his own that had left a ditch full of water behind the chicken house. Everybody worked and suffered that week, and worst of all, when everything was spotless, poor Fillene was invited to stay outside while we went into town after the Sunday paper.

I was looking forward to a morning reading the funnies; Daddy already had the sports section out and ready to go so he wouldn't waste any time getting to the good stuff once we got in the house. As we drove into the garage Fillene was standing on the other side of the screen, in the kitchen, wagging his tail—I thought I had put him outside—I did put him outside before we left. How? And then I saw his feet, his sides, his tail—most of him was not black any more but different shades of yuck.

The minute she saw him Mother bailed out of the car, tore through the kitchen, and started screaming,

"My house! My beautiful house is ruined!"

And it was. Fillene had taken a mud bath in Daddy's ditch, torn open the screen, then turned cartwheels and jumped from couch to couch, skidded on the waxed floors, and slung mud on woodwork and windows and curtains. Then he crawled on top of my bed and rolled from one end to the other, evidently ran out of mud, dashed out for more, came back through the screen in the guest bedroom, and was just about to jump on the pure white bedspread when we drove into the garage, since there were skid marks on the new carpet and one paw print on the bedspread, then tracks leading out through the kitchen to the porch.

Mother sat down on the couch, mud and all, and didn't say anything. She'd open her mouth but nothing came out. Daddy had already grabbed Fillene, and they were on their way out of the house. I could see Fillene's tail hanging down between Daddy's legs as he dragged him out. It wasn't wagging anymore. The funnies and the sports section didn't get read that day.

Daddy still talks about Black Sunday. That's when Fillene starts studying an ant crawling someplace and acts like he doesn't understand people talk. But I know he understands everything except what made him do what he did that Black Sunday.

Bandito

"No more huskies, and that's an order!"

Daddy's mouth was thin and tight and his eyes—squinting darts. Not all the begging in the world was going to talk Daddy into letting me have that cute little puppy. The two huskies that came before had not been very happy on our hill in West Texas—too hot, too dry, too far from the North Pole I guess. But this one had no place else to go but home with me. I put her into Daddy's arms and told him how Angie's daddy was transferred to Houston, and they'd have to live in an apartment, and they wouldn't allow pets at the apartment and this poor little puppy would have to be put to sleep and . . . Daddy rubbed her behind the ears, gave her a little squeeze, and said, "Oh, all right."

So Bandito joined our family on the Hill. I named her Bandito because she wore a mask just like Posse did. Her eyes were like blue ice and I never could tell what she was thinking.

First thing, she got real sick. The vet said she had a bad virus and to keep her away from the other dogs. His warning came too late for Tootie and Fritzi and Winnie. They were older and I guess that's why they weren't as sick as Bandito, but it looked like a hospital around our house for a long time. Bandito finally got well but Daddy thinks her being so sick affected her growing and thinking. She was never very tall and I couldn't teach her anything. We thought Posse had been hardheaded. But Bandito's head was solid rock. Finally, Daddy said something had to be done with her. She needed to go to school cause she was "incorrigible." I sure learned what "incorrigible" meant and even how to spell it!

Bandito went away to school. She was to be gone for six weeks, learning how to "heel" and "stay" and "fetch" and other stuff she needed to know to be a nicer dog. Even I noticed how peaceful the Hill was after she left, how much happier the other dogs were, and Daddy didn't fuss and growl so much. He called every once in a while to see how Bandito was doing and each time he'd hang up, shake his head and say, "That dog." One morning Bandito's teacher called and told us to come pick her up. Daddy asked why so soon; she wasn't supposed to come home for another two weeks. I don't know what the lady said, but Daddy slammed down the receiver, grabbed his keys, and told me to come too 'cause Bandito had been thrown out of school.

Bandito and the teacher were sitting on the porch, waiting for us. She marched out to the car dragging Bandito on a leash. The teacher's face was red and sweaty and she was almost hissing like a rattler. She told Daddy, "Don't ever let this dog have puppies!"—that she couldn't sleep at night knowing there was more than one Bandito in the world—that in all her years of training dogs she had never run into one like this—that she wasn't going to charge Daddy a penny 'cause he had enough problems just owning "this one." Then she opened the pickup door, stuffed Bandito in, marched back to her house, slammed the door, and was gone!

Bandito looked up at me with her empty blue eyes, crawled into the seat between us, and said she was ready to go home.

The Hill Gang wagged their tails and barked as we pulled into the driveway. When Bandito stuck her head out and they saw her, everybody stopped jumping and clattering, dropped their tails, and went on doing whatever it was they had been doing before.

Bandito was all mine. Nobody else wanted to have anything to do with her. I was determined to find some way to make her into a good dog. I hugged her neck a lot, I talked to her, I gave her treats, I invited her to do special things, I let her sleep with me, and she STILL looked at me like she had never seen me before in her life! She walked off while I was trying to hug her. She used the bathroom wherever she got the urge—my rug, my bed, the living room floor. She would not "come" or "stay" and certainly wouldn't "fetch" unless it was the Thanksgiving turkey Daddy was supposed to come in and carve, or the chocolate cake Mother had set out to cool on the counter top. She ate a whole box of my chocolate covered cherries. I didn't know what had happened to them until I found where she had thrown them up under my bed. That did it! Out she went, never to come into the house again. Daddy would be so upset about Bandito he fussed about her to his buddies at the coffee shop, how bad she was and that we couldn't do anything with her or about her. He said everyone around the table shook their heads and stared into their coffee cups—everyone except Karl Kulhanek, who owns a junkyard of wrecked cars and broken-down farm equipment. Karl said maybe Bandito was just what he needed to stay in his junkyard and scare people from breaking in when he wasn't there. Daddy said he sort of tried to talk him out of the idea, but he didn't want to try too hard.

That's where Bandito lives now. Every time we go by Karl's junkyard, there she sits with all that rusted, rumpled stuff around her. She has the same look on her face she had when she sat on top of my bed.

All
American
Dog

Curley

Glowing coals popped and cracked as Daddy and I tossed pecan hulls into the fireplace. The day was cold and gray and I had to ride the school bus home cause Daddy needed to get the animals ready for a big freeze that was supposed to happen that night. The weatherman said the wind chill would be at minus eleven by the next morning. We had been shelling pecans ever since it got dark, so I was real glad when a horn honked and the shelling could stop, for a little bit at least. Daddy went outside, stayed a long time, but when he came back in he had a black and white border collie on a leash. That was the first time Curley and I met. Daddy said Ben Stowe, our neighbor about two miles over, brought Curley to us till things warmed up. They were planning to stay in town till the thaw set in, so nobody would be at his place to keep the ice broken on the tank for Curley. Besides that, Curley was a people dog and needed to be around folks. The tanks thawed, the wheat sprouted, the birds built nests, and Ben Stowe never got his dog back. Oh he'd come get him, take him home, but a couple of hours later Curley would be back wagging his tail at our back door. Full grown dogs usually stay put, so we never understood why Curley wanted to move in with us, but I'm still living and breathing because he did!

• • • • • • • •

Miss Simpson, my teacher that year, asked us to capture bugs and put them in fruit jars and bring them to class so we could show and tell; that way we'd know all about the good ones and the bad ones before summer came. I had bugs in shoeboxes and jars, and I managed to get a whole ant hill in a bucket. Daddy walked into my room to look at my collection, saw the bucket of ants and said the ant hill had to go, "Now!" he said. So I hauled the bucket out of the house, down the driveway. There was still enough daylight that I could see where I was going, I thought. Curley ran up to help. He nosed around, sniffed at some rocks and weeds and things.

I figured I was far enough away from the house to dump the bucket, and besides that some of those pesky ants had escaped and crawled up my arm. Next thing I knew Curley nearly knocked me over, planted himself square in my path, and wouldn't let me by. He was really on a tear—barking and barking and not moving out of my way. I got so mad at him I told him to move over and let me by, but he didn't budge. He just stood there, legs spread out like a sawhorse, swishing his tail in my face barking and snarling and growling and barking. Daddy turned on the outside lights and ran out hollering, "Don't move! Don't move!" I didn't! Curley was standing right smack between me and a rattler as big as a fire hose. The snake was hissing, swaying its head back and forth, and shooting out its tongue at him.

Curley made every move the snake did, barking and barking, lunging and barking—then the snake got him! By that time Daddy was there with his pistol. Pow! Pow! He grabbed me up, hauled me to the house, dumped me behind the screen door and ran back for Curley. By then it was really dark; the light from the porch didn't go far, but I could see Daddy on his knees, talking to him, trying to get him back to the house. Curley wobbled, but he was walking. His face looked kinda lopsided, like he had a mump. That snake had bitten him on his face, and he would die because of me and those silly ants! Daddy called the vet, talked a little bit, and then hung up. He stroked Curley's back and talked to him, thanking him over and over for keeping me away from that rattlesnake. Poor dog wasn't paying much attention because his head was getting bigger and bigger, and Daddy was worried about that. He said there wasn't any use in taking him to the doctor. There was nothing he could do. Since he was bitten above the heart, other than a sore head, he'd be all right after the swelling went down. If he'd been bitten below his heart, there wouldn't be anything anybody could do either. He'd just have to die.

Curley lived with his big head for several days. He slept on my bed with me. He didn't have to get off except to go to the bathroom. Even with all that attention, breakfast and suppers and goodies in bed, Curley never got spoiled; in fact, he acted kinda embarrassed about all the nursing I gave him. But he got well and was as good as new, except for one thing—he hated snakes! Daddy said he'd be a good snake dog after being bitten. And he was; Daddy was right.

Curley prowled the Hill looking for anybody that didn't belong there—snakes, skunks, raccoons, armadillos, possums—

he wasn't even afraid of taking on badgers. When the moon was full the coyotes howled and screamed and hollered, and Curley did lots of barking to let them know not to come into his territory. Daddy had explained about the "territory" and how important it was to animals and birds and things. They respected each other's territory most of the time, and when they didn't there was usually trouble—like when I got into Daddy's toolbox, I was in Daddy's territory, and then I usually got in trouble.

That night Curley wouldn't stop barking, even though Daddy went outside and made all kinds of threats if he didn't shut up. I stood out on the balcony and watched Daddy and Curley. Daddy fussing, Curley barking, stopping, turning around to make sure Daddy was still there, then barking and creeping down the Hill a little more each time. All the noise seemed to come from the same spot at the bottom of the Hill. Then Curley rose up out of the bushes with a bunch of shadows circling around him. They were taking turns jumping and nipping at him; he whirled and danced around, all the time working his way up the Hill toward the house where Daddy could see them. Daddy fired a shot into the air and shadows darted away in all directions, leaving Curley standing there by himself. One single shadow dashed across his path; then all was quiet. Curley stood like a statue for a few minutes, then he let his ears down, wagged his tail, trotted over to Daddy, and licked his hand. He flopped down on the decking and went to sleep.

Curley spent his days and nights doing brave deeds, and all the Hill Gang looked at him with great respect and appreciation. He never acted proud or snooty or spoiled, and when he was placed to rest in our dog cemetery my daddy painted a marker that said, “Here lies Curley, the ‘All-American Dog.’”

Mr. P

Except for the Herrings, who came to feed the animals and water the plants, no one had been on the Hill for over a month. We went to New Mexico and Colorado looking for cooler weather and hoped by the time we got home in September that summer would be over. Besides, school started the day after Labor Day. Daddy unloaded the car, but I needed to check out back and make sure everybody was okay in the dog yard. I opened the back screen and almost stepped into a pile of bird doo. There were a few white feathers scattered around, and when I looked up there sat a big white pigeon on the edge of the roof looking down at me! He didn't flutter a feather or make a move except to bat his eyes at me like I had no business being in my own backyard. I didn't move either; I just gawked—pure white against the pure blue sky—some kind of sign from heaven! I eased back through the door, carefully closed it, tiptoed down the hall, and whispered as loud as I could for Daddy to "come see! Come see a beautiful white bird from heaven on OUR roof!" I needn't have worried about scaring him away. He had come to stay for a while.

Before we left on our trip to New Mexico, Daddy took off a closet door and stood it up on a wall outside the door till he could get it fixed. That was Mr. P's new home, and after he made our acquaintance he hopped to the top of the door, stared down, and just dared us to do anything about moving it. We didn't.

What did pigeons eat? Well, I gathered up all kinds of crumbs and made crumbs out of all kinds of things and put the dish out for his dinner pan on a patch of shaded grass. He wasn't going to eat on the grass. Daddy said that he was too smart to do that. We'd have to arrange for him to have his meals upstairs, he said, or he wouldn't be eating at our house. So the next time Mr. P (I named him Mr. P, short for Mr. Pigeon) flew out for a stroll, Daddy had his ladder ready, climbed it, and nailed one of Mother's pie pans to the top of the closet door. I couldn't find enough crumbs for the next meal so we went to the feed store in town and bought a proper diet for Mr. P, at least that's what Mr. Evans at the feed store said. It sure looked dry and seedy to me. We filled Mr. P's pie pan. He landed right in it, walked around, scratched and pecked and when he got full or tired he just plopped on top of what was left of his supper and went to sleep. Since most of it was gone the next morning, we figured he approved of his new menu.

When the northers started rolling in that fall, Mr. P never complained. He just sat in his pan staring into me, never moving, but he puffed his feathers out so full his eyes didn't show. One night the wind blew so hard and made such noise that we didn't hear the door fall down. The next morning Mr. P's perch was on the ground and he was on the roof looking down on us with complete disgust. Daddy got out his hammer, nails, and boards and built a shelf right under the roof, nailed the pie pan to it and put a board on the side to sort of break the wind. We hoped that Mr. P wouldn't leave us because we had changed houses on him. When he came back after his afternoon flight around the Hill, he landed on the pie pan, ate a few seeds, closed his eyes, sort of half opened them, blinked "thank you," and went to sleep. Since we were watching from inside the door, Daddy said, "You're welcome, Mr. P," and winked at me. Thank goodness he liked his new home!

That year, the last I was home before TCU, the snow started falling the day after Christmas. Sometimes it snowed, sometimes it sleeted; sometimes it rained and formed on the windowpanes in swirls and splotches. I could see Mr. P through the whirling crystals of ice and snow, sitting on his perch all puffed out like a huge coconut cookie.

Mr. P never flew away when I wanted to visit with him. He listened politely and fluttered a wing, dipped his head, gargled a few words sometimes, but I never touched him. How I wanted to pet him—just one little pet! I'd climb the ladder, hold out my hand, but he'd either hop over or fly away. He kinda hurt my feelings, not wanting me to hold him or anything. As the days turned warmer, he left his perch and strolled through the grass below, pecking and scratching, making pigeon songs as long as no one was outside and there was no danger of dogs to bother him. Daddy and I made sure the dogs didn't ever get to know Mr. P.

• • • • • • • •

Mr. P didn't want to fly anywhere but around the Hill. Usually he made one or two turns and then he came right back to his home. Sometimes he went for days not going anywhere or doing anything; he just sat, ate, slept, and stared off into space. I wondered what he thought about all the time.

Daddy took me to Olney one afternoon not long before school was out for the summer. I climbed into the pickup and we headed down the Hill through the pecan orchard, and on to the highway to town. I wasn't in a hurry and Daddy wasn't either, so we were poking along. A shadow flashed across the hood of the pickup and then back across. Daddy slowed down as much as he could and we turned our heads, looking in all directions to try to see what was making the shadow. There was Mr. P! He swirled and soared and swooped down so we would be sure to see him. He had never done this before. I hollered and told him, "Go back home!" Well, he dropped down right in front of us, dipped his wings once on each side, and shot straight up into the clear blue sky until we couldn't see him anymore! Daddy didn't say a word, but he was swallowing hard 'cause I could see his Adam's apple bob up and down. I didn't talk about it either—maybe sometime later I would, but not just then.

I see Mr. P lots of times when we travel down a road. Daddy says all the white pigeons I see couldn't be Mr. P. Daddy still climbs the ladder every so often to put fresh food out, and we still look for him to come swooping in to tell us he's home again.

Epilogue

Mother and Daddy still live on the Hill. I do too part time, since I am in college now and I only get to go home on holidays. But I haven't filled my head so full of "learning" at TCU that I could ever forget about my doggies, not just the ones I told you about but all the others that have passed through my life—Tiny Tim, Dusty, Caleb, Igor, Jackie O, Char, Angelina, Peaches, and Lady. Like Daddy said, they all have left a mark of some kind on me without ever saying a word. They have given joy and sadness, fear and pain, comfort and loyalty. Where else could I have learned so much about life—and death? These doggies have been so much a part of my world that it's a wonder I don't bark instead of talk.

Addison and Randolph Clark, the founders of Texas Christian University
Photo courtesy of *TCU Magazine*

Carol Thornton was born in Fort Worth and graduated from TCU. Carol has taught high school English and speech, written plays, squired her students around the state to UIL events, and sprinkled in numerous trips in the US and Europe. After eleven years she decided to switch careers, and she began to sculpt. She opened the Carol Thornton Gallery in Santa Fe, and she had the opportunity to sculpt the founders of TCU: Addison and Randolph Clark. Through the years of challenges, heartaches, adventures, victories, and changes, her dog companions have always been there for her.